Memories,
Wishes and Regrets

Memories,
Wishes and Regrets

Rk Lindsey, Jr.

Copyright © 2023 by Rk Lindsey, Jr.

All rights reserved. No part of this book may be reproduced in any form or by any electronic or mechanical means, including information storage and retrieval systems, without permission in writing from the author and publisher, except by reviewers, who may quote brief passages in a review.

ISBN: 978-1-961096-47-9 (Paperback Edition)
ISBN: 978-1-961096-48-6 (Hardcover Edition)
ISBN: 978-1-961096-46-2 (E-book Edition)

Some characters and events in this book are fictitious. Any similarity to the real persons, living or dead, is coincidental and not intended by the author.

Book Ordering Information

The Regency Publishers, US
521 5th Ave 17th floor NY, NY10175
Phone Number: (315)537-3088 ext 1007
Email: info@theregencypublishers.com
www.theregencypublishers.com

Printed in the United States of America

Contents

Dedication vii

Rk Lindsey, Jr. Memories ix

Memories 1

Wishes 45

Regrets 49

DEDICATION

Dedicated to my favorite cousin Reginald Earl Lindsey.

RK Lindsey, Jr. Memories

I have a basket of **_memories_**, **dreams and regrets** swimming around in my head from bygone days, to _hukilau_ (pull in) from the tangled net in my neanderthal brain to sort through. _Hukilau_, a net bubbling with fish, destined for a barbeque grill at a Hawaiian luau, being dragged to shore from the sea.

Psychologists claim seventy thousand thoughts, swim through our mind every day. Every day. Can you believe it?

You've heard the Hukilau (mele) song at Hawaiian events. It's a popular _hapa haole_ (Hawaiian, meaning half Caucasian) song.

Last evening, I strung my net out at the Mauna Kea Beach Hotel at Kaunaoa Bay, in front of a lava cave about two feet in diameter facing west. It's my secret _koa_ (habitat) where the special fish I'm after, spend the night, _menpachi_ (soldierfish). The ocean was trembling. The water; murky, cold, nervous. Angry over something. Water, sharks love to lurk in. But _akua_ (God) will protect me. He has for fifty-two years.

Froze my _olos_ stringing out my net but nature wasn't going to stop me. Not even Vladimir Putin. I was, a man on a mission. I know you know what I'm referencing. Both _olos_ were the size of olives when I entered the water. The size of peas when I got out. Needed a Geiger counter to see if my ornaments were still where they're supposed to be.

Strung out the net where Huff's favorite fish, *menpachi* (soldierfish) hang out. Baited it perfectly for the morning *hukilau*. Over the years, I've perfected the 'catch fish' science Huff taught me. The cave where the menpachi as well as other fish, use as their master bedroom. It's my secret spot. And Huff's. He showed me the cavern (*koa*) years ago. Made it clear our secret was to remain our secret. The net is a gift from him as well. Fish can enter, but once in, they're in trouble. There's no way out.

I checked the moon almanac last night as I was watching Hawaii 5-0. The calendar guaranteed me a good catch. Tonight, is the perfect night to pursue *menpachi*. I look east towards Puna. There's *Mahina* (moon), the full moon beginning its ascent. I turn west. And watch the sun fall below the horizon.

Oh, what a magnificent sight. That big ball of light with the man, head bowed, chin resting on his knees, two hundred forty thousand miles away, dangling in the Hawaiian sky. Raining down its soft light on us as we sink our heads into our pillows. And the sun, ninety-three million miles away, lighting, warming up the other side of the world, only to return in twelve hours. Both light bulbs doing what the Creator assigned them to do. Bring light to where there is darkness.

Usually, fishers either pole or spear *menpachi* but I'm using a net. A spear and pole won't do. I need about three hundred. And I sure need the moon's help tonight. I'm sure you've seen the wall plaque. 'Jesus never fails.' We have one on our kitchen wall. It has never failed me. Never! I glance at it occasionally. He took time to visit the Gentile lady by the well. Something he was never supposed to do. I need to be more like him. Listen. With my ears. Not mouth.

I'm up earlier than usual. The wife is snoring and snorting her best. She could blow our driveway clean with the powerful hot air coming out of her cannons. Her nostrils. The noise sounds like turbines on a jet plane ready to fly off to LAX from Keahole Airport. I was going to shake her up to cook me breakfast but thought best not to.

So, I cook and serve myself in her spotless kitchen. I know I will get some rash later. But I'm one of these guys. A duck with a strong back and two deaf ears. Noise in. Noise out. I scramble four eggs and sausage. Throw them on a plate over two scoops of rice. Douse my meal with oyster sauce and shoyu. Pour me a third cup of coffee minus creamer, this time. Slice a papaya in half. Turn the kitchen radio up to buffer 'the oink oink music' coming from the master bedroom.

I'm in pig heaven. Eat my best. Now I'm coffered out. I can't wait to drive down to the bay to inspect my net. I leave a big mess in our tiny cafeteria. Egg and papaya shells on the counter. Don't want the noise from the disposal to wake the old lady up. Now isn't that thoughtful? I leave my coffee cup, utensils and frying pan in the sink. Splattered oil on her once immaculate stove. No time to towel the oil off. I'm on a tight schedule. The clock over the sink tells me I'm ten minutes behind schedule. I hate to be late. It's one of my insane allergies.

Sometimes I must give the wife something to grumble about. I don't believe in the 'happy wife, happy life' doctrine. I look at life this way. Life should be a mix of peaks and valleys for the valleys to be appreciated. Contrast is the middle ground between bad times and good times. Between rose with thorny stem and cymbidium orchid you can squeeze without pricking your hand. I like my metaphor. Could have used it in English class in high school where I usually got D-'s and F's. May have raised my grade some. D to C+. Almost flunked high school because of Miss 'English' (fictitious name). She gave me a D just to get rid of me. Miss 'E' was the kind of teacher I wanted to put a board with twenty twenty penny nails nailed through it under the comfortable cushion she sat on as she read "Romeo, oh Romeo where you stay?" to us as if we were kindergarteners. I would have turned her chair into an ejection seat and rocked her buns. She would have hit the ceiling only to fall into Romeo's loving arms. A bad memory revisited.

Gosh I need to clear the negative toxins out of my head. And look to the future not the past. 'Get thee behind me Satan.' I'm easily distracted. Suffer from ADD. How about you? Especially in the morning when I'm in a rush and not thinking pure thoughts. Not thinking straight.

Rolling forward. Today may be feast. By a long shot. Maybe A*lahs* (famine). I will soon see what's in my *eke* (net). I wish I could say I'm a forever optimist but that would be a lie. What's in my head is in my life. I need to change things around. Read this in a book recently. Our son gave it to me. Think he's sending me a 'you are what you think' message.

E pluribus unum. I have full and complete faith in the puppeteer yanking my chain from upstairs. And of course, *mahina*. In life, you must be. Otherwise, why exist! Why spend life pouting, grumbling, judging? Life's too short to be a skeptic. You're here today than in a flash, 'Gone to Maui.'

I strip off my pj's. Put on my favorite shorts. Grab my coolers from the garage. Ten filled only with ice. Two with beer on ice. Load them in the back of old Rusty. My snazzy looking truck. I think it's snazzy. After thirty years, it's showing its age. Rusted out from salt air and full of holes because we spend a lot of time at the beach. The wife wants me to buy a new truck. She says Rusty is an embarrassment. To her but not me. We live in a gated, high-end community. With the kind of people who 'think they are better than thou.' I want to move out, but my poor dear doesn't. So 'woe is me.' I'm stuck between a rock and a rock. She and the association are on my case. They've sent me two subpoenas which I trashed. Big …… deal! They can grouse all they want. Rusty is my pal. I will not get rid of him until he says he wants, needs to go to the 'boneyard.'

I grab my flippers and goggles, handbag with my special t-shirts, crank Rusty up. He purrs like a Persian cat. I gun the engine several times. I love when he backfires. That means he's alive and ready to greet the day. We can't have roosters. The association rules only allow poodles. Rusty is my rooster. Rusty is my poodle. The neighbor across the street is pulling mail out of his mailbox. He yells at me and flips me off. Guess he had a bucket of rusty nails for breakfast. I curse him, give him some sign language and drive off. Rusty sounds so good. He can use a tuning. Maybe the next time we're in Hawi.

My beloved dog Skippy wants to tag along. I see him chasing us in my rear-view mirror. I stop and he jumps through the open passenger door window. We're off to Kaunaoa Bay. "What you think Skippy? Am I going to be disappointed?" He barks three times, which means, "Hell no." I give him a treat, a reward for his confidence. He's been my buddy and confidant for twelve years. The association is bitching about him to because he's not a poodle. But to me, he is.

Compared to last evening, the sea is a polished mirror. A warm breeze blows in from the northeast. It's a 'see forever' day. The sky is crystal clear. Skip and I swim out to the net. The water is warm. It feels so nice and sensuous. My *olos* are soft and fluffy. I tug on the net. I've hit gold. It's fraught with menpachi, manini, couple eels, some rubbish fish, yellow tang. My ROI is off the charts. The net is heavy. Tons of fish are flapping their tails like Skippy does, when he's ecstatic. I look over. Yep. His tail is spinning like a Ferris wheel. A school of *opelu* and *halalu* swim between my skinny legs.

A bunch of friends show up to give me a hand. I couldn't *hukilau* by myself without getting a hernia. I need their help. A group of strangers also jump in. We laugh and chatter, huff and puff, as we pull the catch to shore. It's a one-sided, unfair tug of war, lasting about a half hour. I don't want the net to tear for obvious reasons. Mending a net is a hassle. So, it takes longer than usual to get to shore and thankfully the ocean bottom is sandy. The net will not be injured at all. Whew!

The fish is for a luau Willow, and I are putting on for grandpa, Huff. Huff the Magic Dragon. Huff Jacob Wilmington III. Huff is pushing eighty. He's a young eighty, married a woman fifty years younger, earlier in the year which ticked me off. On New Year's Day. "Why are you marrying that thing?" I ask? "I still have smoke coming out of my chimney. And she makes me happy." "She's going to conk out your heart is what she's going to do." What he does is none of my ......business. I know that. But this broad is a gold digger. I tell him she is going to milk his chimney dry. Plus walk off, with all the gold in his mouth. And find herself another chimney for a pacifier.

But I was wasting my time trying to protect him from himself. I love the guy. He helped raise me up when my parents died in a plane crash coming home from Spain. I was four. Took me in and made me a man. I was the kid, he and Bea never had. He was an only child and so was I. I idolized him and was renamed, Huff IV. He could fly a plane, drive a forty-foot boat, sail, operate a motorcycle like Evil Knievel. And boy is he a prankster. Wanted to send me to the best schools. I wanted to go public. So, I did and have no regrets. I didn't need to work. I spent life with him doing what he wanted to do. He had money coming out of his pores. And I did my darndest not to help him spend it. He didn't need help anyway.

In my younger days he was 'Pops.' When he turned sixty, he was 'Papa.' Now it's back to 'Pops.' Bea was always 'Ma.' We lost her five years ago. Died in her sleep unexpectedly. Pops and I cried like babies at her service at St. James. I had never seen him cry before. He refused to let the mortician and priest wheel her casket out of the church. Held up the service for two hours. I finally convinced him, we had to let her go. He was a big man. Hung on me the entire time. After she was buried, we sat by her grave for a couple hours. I felt terribly sorry for him. And for me. She was our rock for so long, a lifetime, brought us so much joy and strength. She's the woman described in Proverbs 3.

The net is in shallow water now. One in the group, a tree hugger type from the Pacific northwest yells at me. "What in hell are you going to do with all this fish? Feed the entire island? Or just take what you want and dump the rest?" I laugh at him. I know my laughter offends him, but I don't really care because I was more than ready for the question. "No. We only need a third of the catch. The rest will be released. Let go." "I see." "My policy has always been, take what you need, give the rest back to the ocean. That's the ancient way." "Ah, makes good sense to me. I like that."

The sun is now at about nine o'clock. It's getting hot. I pull out the fish I need for the luau. The rest are let go. "Why don't you take everything?" a stranger walking by asks? Here we go again. Redundancy, but it's an appropriate question. A teachable moment. I repeat myself. "Here, we only take what we need. We know when enough is enough."

I ask a buddy to clean the net and hang it out to dry. We put three hundred *menpachi* in coolers filled with ice. Now is the fun part. Gutting, scaling, cleaning. With all the hands I have, the work goes quickly. Soon, we run out of beer.

"Can someone turn water into beer?" "There was a time when I could," a clown from Tacoma chirps. "But I lost my *mana* (spiritual power)." He's got a local connection. I like that. "How in hell did that happen?" I ask. "Lose my *mana*?" "Yeah!" "I met Eve. She …… things up. The python tempted her to pick the fuji apple. She took the dare. Got us evicted. You guys know the story. First, we moved to Memphis. Then Philly. Seattle. Now Tacoma, but I think we'll pack our bags and move here. I like Hawaii" "Why?" "I like the slow life." "In time it might be too slow." "If and when that happens, we'll just move on. Tahiti maybe." We laugh at the joker. He's a big talker and a moment like this is a refresher for me. The world is made of all kinds. "Red and yellow, black and white. Fat. Skinny. Hairy. Hairless. We are all precious in his sight."

Someone went to get more beer, mahimahi sandwiches and chips. I remind everyone to take it easy, we have a luau at the golden hour for my Uncle Huff. They're all invited. Wives, kids, significant others, dogs, whoever they want to bring. Skippy is sitting on my lap. He agrees, licks me on my chin, barks three times.

We sit in the shade of a coconut grove and out pour more stories and memories. There's too many of us. One guy from Portland, says he caught the biggest marlin. Two thousand, three hundred one pounds, fourteen ounces. Another, this dude from Milwaukee claims he did. How much did it weigh? He didn't know.

It got away. The line broke. He pulls a photo out of his wallet. We take a vote. He has no real evidence to support his memory. The photo is insufficient. His arc of history is tossed in the bull shit bucket. Folks start to rag him. I look at him. He's not happy. Finishes the beer in his hand, curses under his breath, walks off. The ragging continues. I chase after him and do my best to bring him back. "No! I need some space. I'm pissed. I don't deserve being a 'tar baby.'" He promises me, he'll be back for the luau. I remind him of time, location and "Don't forget to bring your wife and kids." The day goes on. Story after story. Memory after memory. Yarn after yarn. We're done and go to wherever to clean up.

The party is informal. Aloha shirts and shorts for us guys. Muu's for the ladies. Timing is perfect. It's an hour from sunset. Everything is in place. We're ready to party.

The maintenance crew setup the stage while we were cleaning fish. The technicians have the wiring, speakers, all the tools for the musicians in place. A group of lady's lug in pots of plants, beautiful bowls of flowers and three strings of leis for the VIP's. Huff, his chickadee, my wife. I made it clear. No lei for me. The bar is ready. The *imu* crew carefully opens the stone pit, they fired up six hours ago to lay the pig and potatoes in. The roast pig smells great. I walk over, a crew member sneaks me a piece to taste. I give him a thumbs up. The servers arrive and verify all they need is ready. Today, I have another memory to tuck away in my photo album of new friends made and a catch up with old friends, I've not seen in a while.

Ah, I say in my mind. We started the morning with a perfect hukilau. Now, we will end it with a perfect evening. The musicians warm up. They play several songs I love. 'Kaulana Na Pua.' 'He Will Carry You.' I sit at a table. Lose myself in the music. Lose track of time. 'Days of My Youth.' 'E Ku'u Morning Dew.' 'All Hawaii Stand together.' I do a final walk through. All is right with the world.

My cell rings. It's Willow aka Kathy. "Aren't you coming home to shower? You must smell like fish." I did smell horrible earlier, and I really didn't care. "I showered and dressed here." "Good. Is everything set up?" "Everything is set up perfectly. You'll love it. I know you'll love it." "I'll be there in five minutes. What shirt are you wearing if I may ask?" "My special shirt." "Oh my God. The one that has FU on it." "Wow, you are smart." "My God. Can I convince you to wear the FBI one?" "Yes, dear. See you soon, my love." "See you soon." Clickety click. The volcano is erupting and as the sun starts its descent, falling to the horizon, because of the thick vog and the cloud bank across the horizon. The sky turns from golden yellow to brilliant orange then ruby red. It takes my breath away. God's magic at work. It's just beautiful. To please my wife. I wear her favorite t-shirt.

Pops is pleased. I'm happy he's happy. The guests. Joe and Frank, old friends still kicking. Everyone's happy. That's sad when you get old. Not many friends left. They start dying on you. The music. I made it clear with the band. No metal suff. Just slow, romantic, beautiful, old suff. They were to play all his favorite songs which they did. The moon lighting up the dark night focused squarely on Huff like a lamp in a concert hall at the Emmy's.

Pops was usually a guy of few words but not tonight. He spoke for ten minutes. I couldn't believe it. **Memory.** Pops tells the crowd; Moon River is the first song he danced with his long-gone Bea at a dance at the Royal Hawaiian Hotel. Says Bea was his best **memory** and how he missed her. I say to myself, 'Pops please don't fall apart.' A memory he says he will take with him to the grave. I look around for his young babe. That was very bold of him to say. She's nowhere to be seen. Nowhere. I find that most interesting. The food. He thanks me for including *menpachi*, asks me to stand up and take a bow. Ordinarily I wouldn't but for Pops I'll do anything. Rob a bank. Whatever. **Wish.** He wished Bea was with him to celebrate the moment. She was not there physically but he could feel her spirit and love around him. His voice started to quiver but regained his composure quickly. Kathy was there to help. **Regret.** Again, he said he wished Bea was with him and when she was with him, he should have treated her better. He also regretted missing many of his old buddies who had moved on to their second lives. He acknowledged Frank and Joe. They were the only ones left of what he called his Mafia. Too old now to play even eight holes of golf, a tennis match or a day on his forty-footer deep sea fishing off Black Point. "Now the three of us play bridge every morning, have lunch at the hotel, go home to nap, return to the hotel for dinner and a glass of scotch. Guess that's our day until our light bulbs burn out." He laughs. Then he asks us all to raise our glasses, shout three banzais to the three of them and sing Happy Birthday not to him but to Bea. Typical Pops, always sharing the limelight.

We all have memories, dreams, regrets. Good ones and yucky ones. Sweet and memorable ones. Those we will spit on the ground, rub, crush under our shoes. Hoping never to see them again. Those that make sense and the ones that make you wonder, where the heck did you come from. From the Man on the Moon. The bully at the end of the street. This place called nowhere. More than likely, like me, you've had a taste, near taste of all, something anyway. - Falling out of the sky. - Getting the dog, you always wanted. -Big Albert, that punk shoving you around because you both liked the same girl third quarter of fifth grade. - Drowning in a rip tide at Hapuna Beach which dragged you out to sea. By the time rescue got to you you were already in St. Patrick's CARE, I mean St. Peter's clutches. You did what you were supposed to do. Swim sideways, away from the rip. But it was your time. - Getting an F in algebra. You were sure a B was coming your way. At dinner mom looked at your test score, saw the F. Her eyes quivered. She thought she was going to see at least a C. Did her best to help you out. Put it in her dress pocket. Tried to hide it from the old man. He steps in. "Let me see what you just put in your pocket cockroach." She has no choice. Gives it to him. "One more F and no more private school for you, boy." - The guy you thought was inviting you to the prom takes someone else. The girl you hate. If you had a knife, you'd have taken it out, stabbed her, and said to the judge after pleading 'no contest,' "I just went nuts, judge. I really didn't mean it." Your insanity plea is granted forthwith. - You were certain you were going to make the first team for football but got your legs chopped off. Coach told you you were good looking, had strong legs but a weak mind. - I could go on and on and on. Memories, wishes, regrets never end. Not until we drop dead.

MEMORIES

Oliver Kelly sings one of my favorite memories songs. **Sweet Memories.** I knew him personally and loved the man. Oliver had wonderful talent. He didn't brag. He was not a showoff. Just sang from his heart. His music wrapped around you like a warm blanket. You would have loved him as well. Unfortunately, we lost Oliver in 1995. He was such a nice, likeable, *olu'olu* (humble) family man. Google and listen to his rendition of **Sweet Memories.** Oh, and at the same time, **Purple Raindrops.**

And so, my story goes. **Memories** first, followed by **Wishes,** concluding with **Regrets.** There's no logical sequence to the events attached to each. Why? It's like what occurs in our minds. Our memories, wishes and dreams. In time and space things just flow with age and experience. Sequence is inconsequential. You never know when something will pop into your mind and why. It just does.

MEMORIES:

My mom and dad

Our mom was a tiny woman. She was tough. Her emotions were made of steel. She weighed not more than ninety pounds, was around four feet eight inches tall. Her driver's license said she was five foot six inches. That was bogus but the cop who issued her her license was our uncle. You know how that works. I towered over her. And I'm five six. She was a martinet. The bad cop who ran the entire show in our house. Our dad suffered from strep throat his entire life. Dad was the good cop. If he had a gun, it would have been just a show piece, made of plastic with an empty chamber.

My brother and I were afraid of her, so was he. We know very little about her. Her growing up years. Her family. We never celebrated ma's birthday because she never wanted to tell us when she was born. Kathy (my wife) was able to pull that fragment of history out of her and baked her her first birthday cake when she turned fifty-two. Can you believe that? When she died, we found out why. She was five years older than our dad, though she didn't look it. She went to her grave at Imiola Church carrying sadly a trunk full of family secrets. What we do know is, she was pure Hawaiian and Hawaiian was her primary language. She learned English when she went to kindergarten at Kalanianaole School. That was during a time after Queen Lili'uokalani's 1893 Overthrow when all things Hawaiian were being undone. Maybe DeSantis got the same stupid idea for Florida from reading Hawaiian history. She got whipped for speaking Hawaiian in school. We do know also that her family owned a lot of 'aina (land) in Onomea, but somehow all that land ended up in the hands of the sugar company.

In our house, she was Teddy Roosevelt. Walked around carrying a big stick and she used it freely. Why? We were stupid. Bad boys. We helped ma, become a tai chi master. Education was important to her. She peered over our shoulders like a hawk when we did our homework. She just wanted to be sure we were on top of our lessons. If we raised hell in school, we got a hot massage first from the teacher then a hotter one from Mr. Nakano, the principal.

The 'coconut wireless' worked quickly in Waimea. When we got off the bus at the end of the day. There was the old lady waiting by the eucalyptus tree at our front gate with you know what. As Mr. Kawabata's bus pulled away. All the rubber neckers were given a free tai chi show. Every show was action packed. A thriller.

Hannah (our mom) was sensei. If we tried to run away, the result was worse. Some of us never learn. If we do, it's the hard way. Ben, my younger brother and I were in that category. It's a good thing she didn't know Brazilian ju jitsu, tai kwan do or karate.

When she died the Social Security office didn't have her name on file. SSN never heard of her. She did not exist. Again, Kathy had to step in and play detective as she did for her birthday. Her sleuthing determined; our mom had been using a wrong name her entire life. Once that got resolved she was able to receive the benefits she was entitled to.

My mom wasn't sure about Kathy at the beginning because she was from the mainland. Wasn't sure if she was going to fly the coop at some point. But ma got to love her in time. It really pissed me off, when they tag teamed me. When our mom died. Her wish was to wear Kathy's favorite dress. I thought that was strange. My hunch, that was her way of saying to Kathy, she was sorry about being skeptical about her.

Both our dad and mom died young. Dad was forty-one, ma was fifty-four. So as much as I joke about her. She is our hero, our north star. Raised us to be good, industrious men. We will love her, and her tai chi sticks forever.

Our dad was a good, generous and kind man. He was loved by all. I don't think he had a single enemy. His brothers loved him. All eight. His two sisters adored him. All our cousins said at a family reunion he was their favorite uncle, in open public. In front of all his brothers. When he died, there was standing room only in our church. Even the catholic and Hongwanji priests prayed over him though we were Congregationalists.

Our dad was always working, so we never got to know him as well as we wanted to. He worked construction, crushing rock and driving a dump truck. He left home when it was dark and came home many times after sunset. He left us early. He died on the morning of, May 23, 1963, in Hilo, Hawaii. Sixty miles from home. We were told he was getting better. The malady he had was surrendering. We knew that was not true. He knew better.

Whatever disease he had, was winning. He was losing weight fast. His baritone voice, once strong and clear, was moving in the opposite direction. Getting softer and softer. Like when you turn your stereo knob down. We knew he was living on a 'short string.' That the 'thief was coming...' One thing we were not sure about. When? In the night. Noon. Tomorrow. A month. We never had the chance to say *au revoir, aloha.* The thief came early in the morning. 1:26 a.m. He was here. Then he was being transported from the hospital bed he occupied for seven months to the mortuary. From doctor (Mitchell) to mortician (Mr. Arruda).

Dad was a pleasant man. Always smiling and cheerful. But our mom for some odd reason, was always on his case. It might have simply been envy. He was a hard act to be back of. He could have been the U.S.'s ambassador to the U.N. There was a time when our church hired and fired ministers as one changes underwear. His job was to help ministers and their families move in and move on. He did it in a way that was gentle, compassionate and kind.

Dad loved animals. Ferdinand was his Hereford bull, Duke his boar, Monty his beloved dog. They loved him to death, went nuts when he was around. They missed him sorely when he left us for his mansion in the sky. He had no time to tell them he was leaving. No time at all. They knew something was wrong when he didn't show, to give them breakfast and dinner, tease them, rub their backs, talk to them. He loved them and they loved him.

Well, our mom. There were times when she had the 'hookies.' A few times. He was a handsome guy, so she'd get jealous when ladies gathered around him at church or community events. Real jealous. Something he had no control over. What was he supposed to do? Head for the hills. Stick his head in the ground. Put on a dinosaur mask. Pretend he was blind, deaf, dumb. Be rude. They loved God, loved us and loved Waimea. They instilled in us solid values. Every single 'Fruit of the Spirit.' Insisted we honor the Boy Scout Law and Oath. Insisted we read our Bibles, pray every night, be kind to people, respect our elders. Love our Country. Respect our Flag. Both were God fearing and believed in serving others.

They lived by the acronym JOY. Jesus first. Others next. Yourself last.

My first memory

I don't remember anything from when I was born to age 4. Nothing. Those four years are tabula rasa. My cognitive apparatus didn't kick in until I was five. What I first remember is, my mom bringing a sheet cake and ice cream to school when I turned five after nap time to celebrate my birthday. I was shocked, stunned. It had all the bells and whistles. A frosted chocolate sheet cake.

Our class was small. Twelve kids and we all had a jolly good time. Our teacher, Miss Karimoto was a sweetheart. She and my mom were coconspirators. I'll remember that cake forever. My friends treated me like a king. It had a fence along the perimeter, a cowboy, rope in hand, chasing down a cow. The cake reflected our cattle town. The guy on the plastic horse going after the plastic cow was our idol. When the party ended, I had my mom collect all the pieces. She took them home and gave them a good cleaning. They slept with me for months. My mom gave me my first memory. What's yours?

Sadly, we know very little about our mom and her *ohana* (family). What canoe her family arrived in the islands on, we will never know. Thankfully, we know a lot about our dad's. His family arrived here in 1847 from England. The Lindsey genealogy book produced by a cousin (Rose Mary Duey) on Maui in 1978 is over an inch thick. It is being updated currently and will probably be more than three inches thick.

Dr. Brown

I surmise he was my pediatrician. His office was on Kinoole Street in Hilo. I hated going to the office because it had the heavy smell of alcohol. Plus, I was afraid of vaccinations. My mom on my annual visit would always tell him, she was so glad I was still alive. I think I was eight when I asked her, driving away from the office after a visit, what she meant by that. She told me I was so sickly when I was born, Dr. Brown told her and my dad I was not going to make it. To prepare for me to die. I had an incurable respiratory issue. She had a hard birth having me. So, when she gave birth to my brother, she had him in Honolulu (Queen's Hospital) where she could get better care.

Red Tricycle

I learned this memory also after I was five. When I was around seven. I was a thumb sucker. Both thumbs. My parents were concerned I would never break the habit before starting kindergarten. They were at a loss. My thumbs were my pacifiers. One day Uncle John came by. They probably asked him what they should do. One morning Uncle John had breakfast with us. He brought with him a bright red tricycle and set it on the kitchen table. He told me the trike would be mine, but the deal was, I had to quit sucking my thumbs. Otherwise, he was going to give it to another kid. I quit sucking my thumbs from that day on. The red trike was my panacea. I rode it until it fell apart.

Living a Good Life

All my life I've been chasing this virtue-perfection. in this life. I've come to realize perfection it is an elusive dream, but it compels me to keep 'reaching for the stars,' to be a better person. For some of us, unfortunately it will follow us to our grave. But St. Peter will be at the Golden Gate with open arms to pick us up. Give us a second or even a fifth chance.

Elvis

Growing up and until today, I love music. Elvis is still my King. Cilla Black and the Everly Brothers are a close second. I 'dug' all of Elvis' songs but two. 'You're Nothing but a Hound Dug' and 'Jailhouse Rock.' You're probably thinking, this donkey is 'jammed up,' if you're an Elvis fan too, especially a die-hard fan. Those were two of the songs that were part of his Kingdom. The Kingdom which made him King. I didn't find the shaking, gyrations necessary. Just couldn't stand it. Seemed like wasted energy. But the *wahines* (ladies) loved Elvis' shaking. Can you imagine, to the point where they'd pull their panties off and wave them at him to grab his attention. Guess they had nothing better to do.

To me, it was not cool at all. Being an embivert, I think is what my failing is.

The love songs he crooned. Oh yeah. Sixty years later, many of those sensuous songs are enshrined in my brain. "Love Me Tender," and "The Wonder of You," still fire up my heart strings.

I've forgotten all the geometry equations I learned in Mr. Springer's tenth grade geometry class, every single one. And seventy-five per cent of the vocab words Hugh Clancy taught us in twelfth grade English six decades ago. This is what I remember about Clancy. He was from England, Shakespeare was his hero, teaching English his first love. He was addicted to the subject. Never lost his accent after living in the islands for over half a century and held degrees from Oxford and Cambridge. He assigned us twenty-five words every week and quizzed us. Speaking for myself, the words went in one ear and slid out the other. But Elvis's songs are branded on my frontal lobe; 'Love me Tender,' 'I'll have a Blue Christmas without you,' 'Wise Men Say,' 'The Wonder of You,' 'Tiny Bubbles' and a few others. When that smooth, mellow, full-bodied voice came over the radio, I stopped doing whatever I was up to and went into a trance. No kidding. Scout's honor. I did. If I was mowing the lawn with the push mower, I stopped mowing, laid on my back and spaced out.

My mom didn't like Elvis. She was an evangelical type. Sort of. So, if she was close by and heard what was playing on my radio. She took all the joy out of my thunder. "Turn that damn radio off. You're listening to a sinful man, singing sinful music." I could never figure out what her problem was. But she was the boss. I had two choices. Turn off the radio or give it up. I always chose the road of least resistance.

Now if he was singing 'Amazing Grace,' 'In the Garden,' "Faith of our Fathers,' 'Bless be the Tie,' 'The Old Rugged Cross.' I'm sure she would have appreciated the King and probably bought a plane ticket to visit Graceland or take in his Honolulu concert when he had a fundraiser for the Arizona Memorial. His soul music was the best. Soul was the basis, the genesis for his music. But my ma suffered from 'stuck brain anitis.' I shouldn't say stuff like this about her. She really in her way was a good mom.

I tried and tried to convince her, to give Elvis a chance, but she was so biased against him. Like she was biased against Huck Finn and Tom Sawyer. Another two of my idols. Though she never met them in the flesh, those three heroes of mine gave her the 'hee bee gee bees.' There was no sense in trying to convert her. Once her brain was stuck in mud, you needed a tow truck to pull a tooth out of the front of her jaw and a military tank to yank a wisdom tooth from the rear. It was best to let a dead dog lie in the middle of the road rather "than fight the good fight" as the Bible suggests.

"You don't know what you've got until you lose it."
(ral donner)

Our mom didn't know what she had in our dad until he died. She really missed him, but it was too late. He was gone. I wish we had grief counseling or Hospice in those days. We needed help. She cried for months. My brother and I were twelve and fourteen. We didn't know what to do. How to help her deal with her sadness. Our minister didn't either. She'd cry for hours until she fell asleep at all hours of the day. In our living room and at his grave in our family cemetery. We could not stand it. It took his dying to help her realize what a good man he was to her, to us, our entire family and Waimea, our community. He was special. He'd give you his last penny and the shirt off his back. My brother and I didn't shed a tear when he died. I've tried to figure out why. After all these many decades I've come up with the answer. It's because we remembered the joyful, happy side of him. So, we didn't, couldn't cry. Our mom saw that side of him also. But she handled her grief by crying. She could not hold back the tears. In time things worked out for her. Thank goodness and thank God.

John Kennedy

Politics. John Kennedy was my man. I remember going to the courthouse in town when I could vote for the very first time. 1968. I was twenty. His name was the first I put a pencil mark by. "Ask not what your country can do for you. Ask what you can do for your country." Those words are embedded in my brain forever. Did you vote for him or Richard Milhouse Nixon? Just being nosey. I didn't like his performance in the debate. Sorry, I'm being judgmental. That night I dreamt about Kennedy and hoped he would prevail, which he did. What happened in Dallas still pains me. I was in Study Hall when the news came over the intercom, he had been assassinated. I went to a military academy, so we all had to stand at attention while the bugler played 'Taps.' ……..Sirhan Sirhan, that evil name is glued in my memory bank as well.

Side Bar On Elvis

Funny how being judgmental, affects one's sense of self-acceptance. As my mom needs to work on being judgmental towards Elvis, Huck Finn and Tom Sawyer. I need to work on my negativity towards her and Nixon. Now that would make a good Sunday morning homily, don't you think, walking up to the communion bench to accept a cracker and a sip of red wine to clear away the dark clouds reckoned as sin for the day?

Now getting back to **Memories** and Elvis. Just a few lyrics to refresh our minds. 'Memories.' How I love that song. The guys who wrote 'Memories' are geniuses. And Elvis, wow, he sings it like an angel standing on the branch of a maple tree, the colored leaves dripping to the ground with a choir of angels around him, humming, smiling broadly, as he shows off the gift of the voice, God blessed him with.

I dream every night about something. I'm sure you do to. My dad. My mom. My paternal grandpa. My good friend, John Hayashi (he died when we were in first grade), Walter Okura and other classmates, my first birthday cake, teachers I liked and the ones I despised, cowboys, ghosts, Kui Lee, my three years at Kamehameha Schools, what the future will look like for our grandsons in this world gone crazy, my first airplane flight to North America, the Golden Gate Bridge, my wife and on and on.

JOHNNY HAYASHI-my second memory

Johnny and I were in first grade, and we would have been classmates and best friends for the ten years I was at Waimea Elementary and Intermediate School. In our town and our school, that was the protocol. After that we went to Honokaa High School by bus for our final three years. With us, when we started off as best buddies with someone it usually was forever.

The last time Johnny and I saw each other; we were playing kick ball in front of our little post office along the main highway through town at the south block of Lindsey Road and Mamalahoa Highway.

My mom went to get our mail at our little post office. It was about the size of a ten by twelve bedroom. Maybe smaller. A reflection of the size of our town then. Aunty Eva was postmaster.

Memories, Wishes and Regrets

In fact, she just passed away. Aunty was ninety-nine and a week short of her hundredth birthday. Then ma went to John's family's store to buy a few items. Probably a pack of cigarettes, loaf of bread and a bag of poi. When she showed up, I knew it was time to go. We waved and said to each other, "See you tomorrow. "Tomorrow" for Johnny and me, never came.

When we got home, about ten minutes later, the phone rang. Those were the days of crank phones and party lines. When others could listen in on your conversation. And spread gossip from Lakeland to Lalamilo and even as far as Hilo. One of my auntie's worked the switchboard. Poor dear. She was always accused of being the town gossip. Truth is. she was. My mom picked it up. The conversation was short. When she put the phone back in the gigantic receiver on the brown box, she had tears in her eyes. I knew something was wrong. It took some doing to make her cry. In fact, I think this is the first time I ever saw her cry. "Poor Johnny!" she muttered. I must have asked, "What's wrong with Johnny?" "He's dead." Having never encountered death before, I know I must have asked," What does that mean?" "He got run over. He's dead." I still didn't know what in hell 'dead' meant. We were planning to play kick ball in school the next day so what did 'dead' have to do with Johnny, kickball and tomorrow. I soon found out. It took some doing on my mom's part to explain things to me. Like when our cat or dog died, we dug a hole, buried and covered the poor dear with dirt. Johnny was gone. We weren't going to be kicking ball, riding swings, playing chase master. All the fun stuff we used to do together. He was gone. Gone forever.

Johnny's ball had rolled under Dr. Black's car. Dr. Black was our town doctor. While retrieving the ball, the doctor not knowing, Johnny was under the vehicle, drove off and dragged Johnny several hundred feet before realizing something odd was going on. Johnny died of his injuries.

A scandal arose. The doctor's nurse took the hit for him. Why that was necessary until today is a mystery? It was an unfortunate accident, and the Hayashi family accepted it for what it was.

It was the first funeral I ever went to. I saw Johnny in this little coffin, covered with white netting. The coffin looked more like a bassinet. Johnny was a tiny guy. He was fast asleep. I tried to wake him up. I wanted to talk to him. What's wrong? My mom grabbed my hands and told me to stop touching Johnny. He was cold. My mother and his mom did their best to explain to me, "Johnny will never wake up. He's in heaven now." I must have asked at least ten questions which I'm sure irritated my mom. Like the Elephant's Child in Kipling's tale. Always asking question after question. Getting in trouble as a result.

I remember all these people sitting or standing in the tiny living room crying. I wondered what all the crying was about. "They're crying for Johnny, that's why!" From Johnny's house, my mom took me to school. I'm sure I told everyone Johnny was dead. He moved to this place called "heaven" and we'll never see him again for a long time. I'm know I did. Miss Karimoto, our sweet teacher could not hold back her tears. Some of the kids started to cry along with her. It was an awful time.

I still see Johnny in my dreams at times. We're in kindergarten at recess, pumping on the swing, swinging on the jungle gym, going up and down on the see-saw, riding stick horses. We're five years old. Laughing. Having a good time. Our teacher, Miss Karimoto, is telling us to be careful. I think I dream about Johnny because we were buddies, his departure was so abrupt, and I had no idea that death was not only sudden. It was forever. It took me a long time to understand what had happened to one of my best friends in the days of his youth. This will sound selfish. It was so unfair. He was taken so soon from us.

His mom in the early years. Soon after he died. When she saw me come into their store would say, "You Johnny's good friend yeah? Come." She'd give me a candy bar or a soda or a handful of bubble gum. "Yeah, Johnny boy, really liked you." I surmise it took about five years for her to work through her grief. After five years, the candies and sodas, quit coming which was okay. She was able to smile and laugh again. Mr. Hayashi, I don't think he ever got over

Johnny's loss. Several years later, tragedy struck again. The family lost another son in a drowning at Hapuna Beach.

Again, this is a book about **memories**. Of days I remember. Bygone days, happy and sad, that will forever be plastered in my mind while I can still remember them. Before dementia, or some other lethal life force, robs me of past times without my permission.

I hope it inspires you to do the same, as a gift to those generations possessing your DNA. Whether you're from Finland, Slovakia, South Africa, the Cook Islands, U.S., Japan, Venezuela or Havana. We all have families we love and adore. Children who are for us rainbows or tornados. Grandchildren we admire. Teachers we remember, for better or worse. Commanders, if we served in the military who were assholes in whose tent, we'd pull a pin off a grenade and give it a roll or good guys we'd charge up a hill and die for. Uncles we liked. Uncles we didn't. I thought I'd start with a sad one and work into others. Do the same. It's not hard. It's easy. Just takes time, and deep thinking. Make a list. A line-up. Dreams. Wishes. Regrets. An outline to work from. And plan to spend hours at the keyboard or a legal tablet with pen and pencil.

My third memory

Dear Miss ..... She taught second grade. Oh, she was a meanie. Always dressed like she was going to morning mass. Wore a scarf every day. Drove a tank of a car. Wore glasses and when she peered at me from under it, I thought I was going to melt. When I say she was mean, I mean it. She didn't have kids and if she did, I would have remembered them in my prayers every night.

I must admit, she treated everyone the same. Miss T believed in gender *equality* when it came to discipline. When we messed up. Did something small to uncork her gourd. She pulled a twelve-inch ruler out of her desk drawer. If we uncorked her major. She got a yardstick off the wall sitting next to the chalkboard hanging on a hook back of her desk. If I remember correctly, she had several sticks hanging in strategic places, so she didn't have to walk far.

They were at her beck and call 24-7. The ruler and the yardstick were edged with metal. She'd stand in front of our desk. "Put your hands on the desk." "Not that way." "Knuckles up." Then 'whop pa.' She scared the …t out of us. She did. It was fun to see her whacking whoever she was. The boy who sat next to me wasn't the sharpest tool in the shed. He tried hard. I mean hard but that didn't help. He would have done well in an alternative school. He was smart with his hands but not with his head. Or had an understanding teacher with a quiet voice, school would have been fun for him. Sitting behind a desk for six hours, five days a week, homework almost every night, was not his 'cup of tea.' I won't reveal his name. If I was in his shoes, I wouldn't want him to divulge my name either.

One day I brought some bubble gum to school. Oh, he really needed to exercise his cud. I dared him to. He took the dare. Guess what happened? She saw him chewing gum, a violation of one of her commandments. Asked him, how he got the gum. He didn't have the guts to rat on me. Said, 'Hayashi Store.' The result. Man, it smelled like a skunk, was paying us a visit. He got 'whop pooed,' sent home and was back in school the next day. I never could get him to take another dare. I tried but my sales pitch failed this time. The other two times when he skunked the room, it was because she was yelling at him. His schoolwork was not up to her par.

I was reading at intermediate school level, first quarter of second grade. I quickly became one of her favorites. Top Gun. She loved to show me off. Like I was a tiger in a circus act. All I needed was a cage pulled by a pony. Not only to my class but to the older kids. Having a second grader read to them. What an insult! I was popular with her but not with some of them. They weren't impressed and wanted to kick my bum, but I had her, her ruler and yardstick, the 'wind beneath her wing' for security. One final item before we go on to third grade. I swear there were times when she came to class smelling like a bourbon bottle. Maybe that's what contributed to her hostility. Ah well, that's yesterday's news. Time to move on.

Mrs. Brand

Like Miss Karimoto, Mrs Brand was a sweetheart. She was the first *haole* (white) teacher I had. Her husband was bookkeeper for Parker Ranch. That was their connection, what brought them to Waimea. The Parker Ranch. As if we didn't have locals who couldn't add and subtract, work an abacus or adding machine. All we were good for was riding a horse, roping a cow and raking poop.

She taught us cursive writing, loved music, reading, poetry. In fact, I credit her for inspiring me for all except cursive writing. Even a chicken can write better than me. I don't have small muscle coordination or whatever it's called. My writing is horrible and the older I get, the worse it gets. Music. 'White Coral Bells upon a slender stock' is the one song I still remember. Poetry. *Trees* by Joyce Kilmer. I always thought Joyce Kilmer was a lady. Only recently, I learned he was a man. It was the first of several poems I learned in her class and remember all the lyrics.

"A poem as lovely as a tree.
A tree whose hungry mouth is prest
against the earth's sweet flowing breast.
A tree that looks at God all day;
And lifts her leafy arms to pray.
A tree that may in summer wear.
A nest of robins in her hair
Upon whose bosom snow as lain.
Who ultimately lives with rain.
Poems are made by fools like me,
But only God can make a tree."

At recitation time I loved how Lillian Kiyota recited it. One of our super smart classmates with a clear, charming voice. She also did 'O Captain my Captain,' by Whitman and 'The Village Blacksmith' by Longfellow. Mrs. Brand loved poetry and that love rubbed off on me from then until today. I haven't seen Lillian in over sixty years and wonder if she is still alive, what is she up to.

After lunch Mrs. Brand would read us stories. Sometimes about my heroes which captivated my attention and dared me to be like them hooligans. Brer Rabbit, Huck Finn, Tom Sawyer. But I was going to be a smart hooligan. Not get caught in the briar patch. If she only knew she was coaxing me to commit a mix of felonies and misdemeanors. If she only knew. She was one of my best elementary school teachers. I failed her in one area. My curse in her class was cursive writing which as I already mentioned only worsened as the years have gone by.

The Parker Ranch cowboys.

The Parker Ranch cowboys were our idols as boys. We idolized them. These guys with Stetsons on their heads, boots, and spurs on their legs, sitting high in fancy saddles, whistling and hollering to and from work. With a dog or two trailing after them. We yearned for the day when our turn would come. When we would be riding the range, working *pipi* (cattle) or participating in the 4th of July Races at Paniolo Park. For some of us it did. Others it was not meant to be.

Waimea School

I loved our little school of two hundred kids. Today, it has blossomed into a thousand scholars. A reflection of how our community has grown. I had great teachers, who gave us a solid foundation for high school and the university. Our parents deserve credit as well. They placed a high value on education. School was easy for me, but I was one of these lazy guys. Did the bare minimum to get by. And get by I sure did. High school and university were a snap. Our school paper was named the Bronco Script. An appropriate name. These are the opening lyrics of our school song. "Lift our hearts in grateful. Raise sons and daughters of Waimea. Swell the echo of our song. Ring it true and clear."

Our school bus.

Mr. Kawabata was our bus driver. He was a very nice, soft-spoken man. Hardly said much of anything to us. Just drove his bus. The bus was an old left-over army bus from World War II. It was still army green though faded and words of caution printed above the windows. He didn't alter it in anyway. It didn't go very fast but got us to school and home safely. One day a punky kid who was new to school and on his first bus ride home started to hassle Mr. Kawabata. He was showing off. For a time, he ignored the new kid. Finally, he could take it no more. The kid began to call him a ……. …. Racist words. Those were fighting words. Mr. Kawabata pulled the bus to the side of the road and walked to the back of the bus. The punk twice his size challenged him to a fight which he gladly accepted. He grabbed the punk flipped him to the front of the bus. Two more flips and …… was off the bus and flat on his … Mr. Kawabata slid back in his seat, and off we went. We learned soon after he was ju jitsu black belt. The punk kid had to walk three miles to and from school after that. Those were the good ole days when you could take the law into your hands. Mr. Kawabata did. No need for a police report. Court date. Judge. Lawyers. Speedy 'kick ass' justice. Problem solved.

Honor's English

Senior year, I was placed in Honor's English. Miss Power's was our teacher. She was going to teach me how to write legibly as she was getting headaches trying to read my writing. So, I had to report to her after school, as she was going to turn things around. It was gracious of her to give things a try. It didn't work. She finally surrendered, told me she was tired of reading my atrocious writing and returned to giving me F's. Thus, I learned how to type with one finger really quick. Which I continue to do. My grade in H.E. thank God went up.

Tutuman

My grandpa Lindsey was a ham. Full of ham. He looked like Santa Claus as he had a thick white bushy beard. I loved listening to his stories which I believed hook, line (60 weight) and sinker.

I would visit him for an hour before ball practice. He saw me wearing my cap, carrying my bat and glove tucked on my bat, slung over my shoulder. That would crank up his story telling engine. He'd tell me when he played ball, he'd hit homeruns from home plate to a bridge five miles away. He was team pitcher and struck every batter out. His pitches (fifty-four) were so hard and fast, the team had to have several catchers to catch his pitches. Their palms got so sore from his throws. He could rope a bull by his horns, neck, belly or feet. If necessary, even by his testicles.

I would sit on the steps of his veranda, mesmerized as he rocked back and forth in his rocker and just eat all he told me up, like a hungry dog waiting for dinner. Then he'd ask me if I wanted to hear him play the piano. I never said 'no.' "Of course." He'd get on the piano bench, rub and warm up his hands, shake his fingers to loosen them up. Thumb through several music books. The first song was always 'Take me Back to the Ballgame' since I was on my way to the ballpark. He'd apologize he couldn't sing because he was recovering from a cold. He used that excuse about five times. Grandpa couldn't sing even if he drank and gargled a five-gallon bucket of lemon juice. He'd play 'Home on the Range' and 'The Yellow Rose of Texas.' I finally had to excuse myself and leave for practice.

He really didn't like kids, but he liked me because he loved my parents and listened to him. When I got home, I'd tell my mom all he told me. She popped my bubble when she said it was all fiction not fact. But it didn't stop me from seeing him. He was lonely, enjoyed my company, and me his.

4th of July

Parker Ranch sponsored on the 4th of July, horse racing and roping contests at the racetrack. As kids, it was a big deal, an exciting time, seeing the Parker cowboys, our idols whipping and urging their horses on. Showing off their roping and tackling skills as well. Than our world changed. At least for a few of us. Military service and the university took us down another path. Took us away from what had always been Plan A.

Brown Smoke

I miss seeing the brown plume of dust from the cattle drives when the cowboy's moved cattle by the hundreds from one paddock to another. And hearing the pounding of the hooves. A memory that is gone forever because the ranch today only exists on paper.

'Aina (Land)

Land in Hawaii is expensive. Our grandpa bought beautiful farmland in the greenbelt in the 1930's for thirty-seven dollars an acre. Today land in the greenbelt sells for a hundred thousand dollars an acre and rising. It's nuts.

Poi

Taro (Kalo) is the foundation of our culture. It represents Haloa, the first *kanaka* (man) of our race. From kalo, poi is made, our primary staple. As a commodity, poi is very expensive. In the 1950's a twenty-five-pound bag of pai'ai (thick poi) sold for two dollars. The poi was so thick it had to be mixed by hand to soften. Poi was sweet and didn't sour back then. Every Hawaiian house had a huge bowl with poi sitting on the kitchen table. Today a plastic bag of poi costs ten dollars. The poi is so soft, it doesn't have to be mixed, you can drink it out of the bag with a straw. Because it is so expensive, there are Hawaiian families, who haven't eaten poi. A sad cultural commentary because of economics.

Hawaiian aloha

"Brah, here let me help you. Come on, no shame!"

Malihini aloha

"God helps those who help themselves."

Campaigning

In 1984 the State of Hawaii went through a reapportionment process as required by law and created a new house district, District 6. I was encouraged to make a run for it. It was primarily a republican district. I was a donkey without a tail. Meaning, no party support, no money in my pocket, no organization, knew no one on Maui to call for help. In short, the Democratic party gave me no help. I was on my own. I had two donkey and two elephant opponents. So, the battlefield was a mite crowded. One of the elephants had money pouring out of his butt. He said he was going to win. I had relatives who told me I had no chance. "Quit while you're ahead." Even my scoutmaster called me to drop out of the race. That really crushed me.

The new district was a canoe district. It included parts of two islands. East Maui and portions of north Hawaii. The cost to campaign in time and money was going to be exorbitant.

With the support and love of Willow and friends, we finally got things together and rolling. The train that once thought it "Could," slowly chugged up the hill to, "Can." I had a Republican Campaign Chair and a lot of republican support ironically. When the general election votes reported out early election night, guess what? We won and handily. My republican challenger was livid. Said it was unfair. I hardly campaigned. He never saw me out campaigning once. Plus, spread lies about me. Said I had connections to the Hawaii's crime Godfather. That was most interesting. Yes, he did.

I want to share with you five interesting moments that occurred while campaigning. First, north Hawaii. We were going to do a grass roots campaign. I had to knock on doors. It was difficult. My strategy was simply to knock on a door, hope no one was home, leave a brochure, move on. Happened a few times. Most of the time people were home and I was invited in to have a glass of water, milk and cookies, even a beer. Progress was slow. Too slow, especially in north Hawaii, because my family is well known. But you gotta do what you gotta do. Second, Maui. I brought a box of campaign stuff and with the help of a friend, met the guy who was going to help in Hana which was the biggest voting bloc in east Maui. He picked us up at Hana airport, it's more like an airfield. We were supposed to knock on doors. Campaign. So, I thought. Because Willow and I had never been to the east end of Maui, he gave us a cook's tour. It's such a beautiful spot. Beautiful. We got to meet his beautiful wife and family. Stopped at the Hasegawa General Store. Met Mr. Hasegawa. Visited Lindbergh's gravesite in Kipahulu. Went to a few other places and met nice folks along the way. The Kuamo'os in Keanae. We did a lot of chatting as he had a lot of questions. He was sizing me up. It was getting late. And I was getting impatient. I finally asked, "Parley, when are we were going to start campaigning." I had made reservations to spend the night, so we could knock on doors, do sign waving. He drove us back to the airport. His reply. "Go home Bob. Hana is yours. No worry." Several weeks later we went back to Maui to campaign in Haiku. Kathy and I drive up to this ranch style house. A pit bull comes out of nowhere dragging this small man. His owner. Attacks our rental car. It must have had a five-gallon bucket of rusty nails for breakfast. It was pissed off. The dog had broken off its chain. The owner grabs what little is left of the chain to restrain it. The dog keeps attacking our car and knocks its owner to the ground. He could not control the dog. The dog keeps sinking its teeth into our car's tires. I drive off and it keeps chasing us. I was afraid it was going to flatten our tires and then what? We'll never forget that incident.

We go to the next house. It's a cute little house, something you see in a storybook. I'm antsy at this point. Worried about a dog coming out of the bushes and chewing on my ankles. I make it to the door. No dog. There's a cat sitting on a windowsill. It meows at me. Wants me to pet it. I give it some time then I knock on the door. No response. I knock again. This tall naked lady opens the door. Stark naked. She's a beauty. Almost like my wife. She's stacked. Like Stormy Daniels. Long legs and arms. Dutch haircut. Blond hair. And a clump of hair, you know where. She knew I was on the campaign trail. My eyes went from the size of a quarter to a half dollar. Invites me in for herbal tea and corn bread. I thank her, "Maybe next time. My wife is with me." "Go get her and bring her in." "Maybe another time." She thanks me for dropping by and assures me I have her vote. She wants several brochures which she'll pass around the neighborhood. That was quite a transition. Angry pit bull to naked lady. In my mind, I ask, 'What's next?'

We do more campaigning and finally reach Paia. We stop at a house with probably forty steps up to it from the road. There's an elderly man sitting in a rocker enjoying the ocean view on a sunny Sunday morning. He looks down at me. Waves me to make the steep walk. He's a kind, elderly man We shake hands. "You're a politician." Wants to know my party affiliation. Democrat. He counters. He's never voted for democrats because democrats only know how to spend money. I hand him a brochure, "Lindsey. Hummm." He wants me to follow him into his house. The place is neat as a whistle. He points to a picture on his mantle. "Who's that?" "President Reagan." "I have to vote for him. You Robert Lindsey?" "Yes." "When Waimea airport was built. I worked with a Robert Lindsey in the quarry. He must be related to you." "He was my dad. He oversaw the quarry." "He was a good man to work for. He was. I tell you what. You get past the primary. I vote for you in the general. You going to be the first democrat I'm going vote for. Not because you democrat. Because of your dad. You nice guy like your dad?" "I try." "Tell him I said 'hello.' My name Manuel. We used to have good fun." I tell him my dad died eleven years ago. He shakes his head. "Au'e. The good ones makeh (die early)."

We get to the airport to catch our flight home. Walking to the gate, a kid is staring at us, "Ma, us the guy." "What guy." "The guy we saw on tv and just heard on the radio. Us him with the *haole* wahine."

Maui no ka oi.

Scouts

I loved scouting. Started as a cub. Den 8. Made it to Webelos. Transitioned to Troop 27. Assigned to Beaver Patrol. Had sights on Eagle. Made it to Star. Our scoutmaster was useless. His assistant, Mr. Hasegawa did all the work. Took us hiking, camping, cycling. The scoutmaster got all the beaver awards which in my book was not fair. My four major memories. **Mauna Kea hike** from Hale Pohaku to the summit. Did the six miles in two hours and twenty-one minutes from Hale Pohaku to the summit and Lake Waiau. Straight uphill. Part of earning our fifty-mile hiking merit badge along with cooking, camping and astronomy badges. No one told us about altitude sickness. Most of the troop passed out on the trail. **Cycling to Kahaluu Beach Park in Kona.** About fifty miles one way on regular bikes. Took almost twelve hours. Flat tires, broken chains, ran out of water because of poor planning, lots of vomiting, those of us who made it all the way, our legs felt like rubber. We were so tired, had no desire to set up our tents, no desire to cook dinner and go for a swim. We just wanted to sleep, and we did under the stars. **Hikes to Spencer Park from Waimea to Kawaihae.** Those hikes were fun. Some of us cheated. I won't elaborate. This was in the 60's before the maddening crowds arrived. We had the entire park to ourselves. Caught fish which we cleaned and cooked. Stayed up all night, played cards, talked about the same stories over and over. Wrestled. Dived off the pavilion roof into a water hole which was not too smart. Oh, what fun we had. We didn't need a one-horse sleigh. **Summer camp at Haena, Ka'u.** We had no supervisor. It was just us. We never went to class, stayed at our campsite and raised cane. We had planned our daily menus ahead of time but ran out of food halfway through the week. Our scoutmaster had to drive almost a hundred miles to resupply us. He was not happy. He earned his Beaver award on that occasion. It was about time he worked for it.

Mr. Morikawa

He was the best teacher I ever had. Well next to Kathy. He had confidence in us. He believed in us; the sky for us was the limit. He wanted us to be the best we could be. We had him for math, ag and general science. We need more teachers today like him. Mr. Morikawa was a committed teacher and brought out the best in us.

First Kiss

I saw her standing by herself on that pleasant Manoa night. She was just beautiful and stunning in her striped, blue pants and turquoise top. I walked over and started chatting with her. I had seen her from a distance twice before. For me, it was 'Love at First Sight.' Got bold, eventually held her close and kissed her. Told her I loved her. I meant it then. And I mean it now. Fifty-three years later. "Until death do, we part." She didn't resist, although my buddy Dennis and cousin Joey, told me she was taken. And, from that point we were on our way. An item. We're still together and still smooching. We have two fine sons, two wonderful daughters in law and four precious grandsons. God has blessed us richly. I wish I had met her sooner. But later is alright to.

Moon Landing 1968

The moon landing really impressed me. I could not believe man, could rocket a spacecraft two hundred forty thousand miles one way to the moon with four guys in it and bring them home safely. I just could not believe it and like millions of others saw it play out on television, led by this guy named Neil Armstrong. Mars is the next target. Wow wee. I won't see it as I will be a can of ashes and dust by then. Just thinking about what is coming blows my mind to Mars and beyond.

Dr. Bernhard Hormann

He was Sociology Department Chair at UH Manoa. Really believed in me and wanted so much for me to pursue a PhD. Served as senior tutor to him as an undergrad. Read and summarized academic journals until I was 'blind.' He planned to move me up to grad assistant, senior year. Dr. Hormann was a gentle, patient and kind man. He was more like a grandfather to me and many others. He liked me because I was Hawaiian. You see, back in the day, if we were both Hawaiian, and smart, we were considered 'exceptional.' Why? We faced a bias. Our lamps didn't burn as brightly as others. We weren't considered scholars in the western sense. I'm glad that has since changed.

Kids

A doctor friend we played tennis with every Sunday, told us, as we were starting out, there's no rhyme or reason to raising kids. We found out how true that is. They're all so individual. All walking to their own drum. Our oldest keeps stumbling, walking off the edge of cliffs. Two are doing fine. Raising, with their wives, great kids, in an uncertain, scary world. Our second son joined the army and ended up in Iraq, early in the war. He was with a helicopter unit. Every time a chopper got shot down and the phone rang from his home station. My hands would shake. "Oh, please God…" It was always good news. But after I hung up, a sense of guilt rolled me. Somebody had lost a son or a daughter, a father or mother. He made it home safely and in one piece. But we lived in fear for months.

Grandkids

They are indeed the pot of gold at the rainbow's end. Two at each end for us. Never thought we'd see the day. Enjoying it while we can. Wish we were younger. I would love to play ball with them. I'm too old and crippled, so I must sit on my fat …watch them, and the world spin by while they kick soccer balls, swing baseball bats, do ju jitsu moves and smack tennis balls. It's so much fun to watch them but it would be even more so being active and doing it all with them. Oh, and yes, sitting in a rocking chair and telling them tall tales to pass on to their kids. How I threw a football ten miles. Hit a homerun into the firepit at Kilauea and Pele, the Goddess of fire caught the skin ball, threw it flaming back to me. She turned it into a fireball. Played 'Jingle Bells' on the piano for them. It was all a hoax, and they ate it up. Maybe in another life. They have the best tutu (grandma). A former teacher, her entire world revolves around them. We were at all their births. All four. She takes them to swimming, piano and tennis lessons. Plays board games and chess with them. Gives them art lessons. Reads book after book to them until her eyes gets so tired. She's fallen asleep on them a few times. When they come by the house, she drops everything she's doing and gives them her entire attention. Games in the cul de sac. When they leave, she's so tired, she has to lay down and rest. They are barrels of energy. Picks and drops them off at their schools when mom and dad are tied up. Never, never complains. The list of how she's helped and nurtured them grow up is endless. I forgot the sleepovers in front of the fireplace. Cups of chocolate. Smores. Meals. Man, these guys can eat. And the popsicles. There are enough boxes in the fridge to last several months. She loves them to death. And they love her to death. Reciprocity in full action.

Second chances

Take care of your health and your family. Got mine in 2016 as I survived a hemorrhagic stroke on a San Francisco visit. I'm so grateful for my wife who has had to put up with so much as a result. Our world has been turned upside down and inside out. ER trips at all hours of the day or night. Falls. Anger fits. Doctor and dental visits. Visits to Honolulu to consult specialists. Visits that chew up an entire day. Starting in early morning to the airport, getting home late at night. Scheduling PT visits. Many a time I acted like a jerk when she gave me good and helpful advice to help get me back on my feet. Advice I should have listened and put in motion years ago. Never once complaining. I'm a lucky guy. A very lucky guy. Another *wahine* would have said 'f..k you,' slammed the door and made damn sure it smacked my butt hard on the way out. I mean it.

Sonny Kaniho

Sonny is one of my heroes. He is a Profile in Hawaiian Courage. He called me out. I said I was for Hawaiian justice. Sonny compelled me to put all my big talk into real action. I wrote a play, a book about him. There are times when I daydream and think about the man. Sonny was a man, a real, good, decent man. He didn't want handouts for Hawaiians. He was too proud. Just wanted what the Hawaiian Homes Act of 1920, a law passed by Congress, to give us that we as Hawaiians were entitled to by law. Lads that were made available by Congress and assigned to the Department of Hawaiian Home Lands to manage and awarded to native Hawaiians, instead were leased to big ranchers. Parker Ranch and Anna Lindsey Ranch (my aunt). A clear violation of the Act.

Richard Smart

Richard Smart was heir and owner, of Parker Ranch. When I met Sonny and agreed to support his effort, Kathy and I lived in Richard's compound. In a small, neat cottage for three years. A cottage built for two. for us. We lived in the Garden of Eden. Our first son was born during this time. I knew when I committed to Sonny, we were facing eviction. Richard was a super nice man. He was hardly around. Was always on travel to the mainland or Europe. He handled our eviction in a classy way. The news had gotten to him. I was a turn coat. Had his secretary, Kiyome Yoshimatsu, call me into his office. We had a friendly chat. Asked how long we lived at Puu Opelu, his homestead. "Three years." He needed the cottage back was his response. Gave no reason. He wasn't obligated to give me a reason anyway. I thanked him for the time we had at Puu Opelu.

We stood up and shook hands. He told me if we needed any help in the future to come and see him. Our rent was $75 a month, utilities free. We lived in a bowl. No one could see us, down a paved driveway about three quarters of a mile long, surrounded by pastureland, grazed by horse's ad cattle. We acted like the entire place was ours since he wasn't around much. The rose gardens were beautiful. There was a 'kiss me quick' hedge on the north side of Smart's modest mansion. At night the fragrance of the flowers was just stunning. At the southwest corner of Smart's yard was a one hundred plus foot Norfolk pine tree. In early December the carpentry crew would string fifty strands of 100-watt bulbs on it. The entire community as well as ships at sea could see it. The tree did its best to add joy to the season. We loved listening to the frogs grumbling in the large reservoir below his home as well as the music of the crickets. We still, all these years later, have fond memories of Puu Opelu and Mr. Smart's kindness. Mr. Smart was the best landlord we ever had. We were sad to leave Puu Opelu. But what had to be, had to be. Parker Ranch unfortunately was leasing thousands of acres that should have been leased to native Hawaiians and Sonny did what he had to do. I was willing to help him and in doing so, it impacted my family. I learned along the way via the congressional record, A.W. Carter, the Ranch Manager, in 1920, went before Congress and lobbied heavily against passage pf the Hawaiian Homes Act because the lands to be impacted were under lease to Parker. Carter did not want to lose those lands. In the end in a sense though Congress awarded those lands to be leased to native Hawaiians because of Carter's political influence, those lands remained with Parker. Sonny messed things up when he showed up in 1974.

Engineering Favorites

1. Electric bulb

I wish I was with Thomas Edison when he made the light bulb and garnered some of his perseverance.

2. Car

With Henry Ford when he made the first 'horseless carriage.' If he only knew how that carriage would alter the world.

3. Toilet

With whoever made the modern toilet. I know the Romans get credit but the guy or girl who engineered the first modern toilet and all that goes with it was a true genius. Taking us from a one sitter over a dirt hole to its own room in a house built for two or three or a football stadium to accommodate thousands.

4. Airplane

With Wilbur and Orville Wright at Kitty Hawk when they made the first mechanical bird out of paper and steel with a prop for a beak and wings with rudders. In time it was greatly enhanced to carry hundreds of people and luggage from Hawaii to LAX or Hawaii to NY.

Roosters crow

We lived in Waimea's greenbelt. A farming area, so everyone had a garden and animals. In the morning it was fun to hear the rooster's crow. Farmers started their day early in our kid days. One rooster would start to belch his crow at around 4 than another and another. A circle of feathered birds singing cock a doodle doo. Our dad worked construction, so he was up early as well. Our rooster would join the circle. Than the Inouye's, the Hirayama's, the Okada's, the Hori's, the Oye's, on and on. You know what cranked them up? The kitchen lights. Whoever turned theirs on first, got their rooster or roosters singing first. And the choir would get going. I miss those days. I'm sure Judas Iscariot, the traitor, does to.

The Kitchen

My bedroom was next to the kitchen, so I got to hear our dad and mom chatting and laughing. Our dad made breakfast on the kerosene stove that warmed up the kitchen while our mom made his lunch. A rice ball with Vienna sausage and eggs or leftovers from dinner or a tuna sandwich. She always made him a big thermos with tea. Sometimes I'd join them and get a treat. A cup of coffee with saloon pilot crackers and butter. That was my dad's idea. My mom said coffee would make me stupid. My dad disagreed. He was right.

Model A Truck

Our dad loved his truck. There was nothing fancy about it. But it took him wherever he needed to get to. The engine was simple. Just an iron block. Easy to fix when it broke down, which it rarely did. Not like today's trucks. You have to be a mechanical genius to solve a problem. His truck didn't have doors. A chain served to keep us from falling out. Today it wouldn't pass vehicle inspection. Truck couldn't go faster than forty miles an hour on a flat road. Going uphill it would sputter and mutter. The bed was just a wood box he hobbled together. The dogs, Ben and I would pile in it when we went into town to do errands or visit Uncle John Kauwe working at his saddle shop, grandpa sitting on the porch watching the world turn or Uncle Jack Puhi at the electric plant smoking his cigar. I believe our mom gave it to one of our uncles when he died. In fact, she gave everything he owned away after he died. Guess she thought it would help her in grieving his loss. It didn't. He stayed in her heart until she died nine years later. She really looked forward to dying because she felt she was going to see him again.

Poha jam

In Hawaii it's called poha berries. On the mainland, gooseberries. We'd collect the berries; our mom would then work her magic. She made the best poha jam. The best. There's no one around today who can make jam like she did, no one. It was a long process, but the wait was well worth it. Poha jam on warm tender crust bread. Ummmm good.

Stealing eggs

We loved robbing the hens of their eggs. They usually dropped their eggs around noon. We knew it because they'd start to cackle. I called that cackle 'bragging.' We had these boxes lined with grass for them to sit on. The back of the box had a special door we opened to collect the eggs. They loved to sit on the eggs after they laid them for a couple hours. My brother and me being impatient became experts at stealing their eggs without them knowing it. We'd slowly, gently work our hands under them and pull the egg out. If they caught us. We'd pay a high price. They'd peck our hand. They wouldn't let go so we'd have to give them some help. Boy did it hurt. I think our batting average was around ninety per cent. Possibly more.

Asato Man

Mr. Asato was an interesting old coot. He owned the ten acres next to our homestead, grew head lettuce, only head lettuce. Asato man was the 'lettuce king' of Waimea. His lettuce heads were the size of cabbages almost. He farmed the old way. With a horse that pulled an iron plow. Delivered his produce to market on a homemade wheelbarrow. If he had to ship stuff to Honolulu, he hiked all the way to the airport, three miles one way, pushing his cart. At times, he made two trips. Always had the stench of sweat and wore a safari cap.

He was a proud man. Didn't speak much English. Japanese primarily. Both he and his wife kept to themselves. I don't think he had any friends. Was a Japanese national. Until the day he died, claimed Japan won WWII. He hated us kids. Didn't want us climbing trees which were mostly on our boundary. A few were on his. Would scream and cuss at us, in Japanese while shaking a sickle. I felt we had to do something about the verbal abuse he was dishing out. Reported to our war room which was nearby. A ginger patch. Me and Ben, my brother. Walter and Clydee, who lived across the highway from us. They said in their tradition, he had to be addressed as Asato man. His screaming and cursing were acts of war. There was no time to appeal to the U.N. or the Hague. We had to act now, so we got our sling shots. Loaded up our pockets with castor beans. Stones would have really hurt so the beans were better to use as ammo. While he and his wife were having dinner, we'd shoot beans through an open window. That would really fire him up. Oh, how that thrilled us. We fired beans until we ran out. Most of the beans pelted their house. In an instant we violated our respect for elders. Became true hypocrites.

They had a son. Rumor had it, without Asato man knowing, his son joined the U.S. Army earning the rank of colonel. Asato man quit farming when his horse died. He was already in his late seventies.

He was a cheapskate. His house didn't have modern utilities. Kerosene lamps to cope with dark nights. Kerosene stove for cooking. Kerosene heater for warmth. Kerosene was cheap. Four cents a gallon back then. Although he had a county water line he maintained a fifty-gallon drum to trap water off the roof (for bathing, drinking, etc.) A one seat outhouse. He kept up with local and world events through a Japanese newspaper. For culture, a crank record player. On still nights, we could hear Japanese music pouring out of the house. I think he and his wife were deaf. It sounded like the singers were constipated. In dire need of a laxative. When he had to phone someone, he used our phone. Our mom could understand his mumbles. We couldn't. Not that we wanted to. That was rare, three times a year maybe. As payment, he'd leave a small bucket of avocados, mutter *arikato* and walk off. Most were rotten. When his wife died, he dug a hole and buried her in it. Someone from the Hongwanji asked him how his wife was doing? He said she died. Her body was exhumed and moved to the church cemetery. The old coot lived simply. Like Thoreau at Walden. Asato man truly lived a life of quiet desperation.

Broke my arm

    I was in seventh grade. Came home from school. Did my chores. Had time to work on my bike. A western flyer. The chain needed tightening. Thought I had the chain fixed. Ma yelled out the kitchen window it was time to take a bath. My uncle David, her brother drives up. They both end up in the kitchen, talking and laughing. I say to myself, time to test my mechanics. I ride off to Orlin's hill where we tested whatever fixing we had to do when we had a problem with our bikes. So far so good. I ride to the top of the hill. Turn my bike around. Ready myself for the real test. The 'proof in the pudding' exam. It's about a forty-five-degree slope, hilltop to main highway. I start pumping as fast as I can go. Halfway down, I brake. The chain snaps and falls to the ground. I'm in big trouble. I can't stop. The bike and me fly past the stop sign at the bottom of the hill. I run into a fence, tumble over it into a ginger patch which helps to cushion me. I hear a snap and feel pain in my left hand. There's a bone sticking out. Waimea didn't have much traffic back then. About a half hour later I hear a car. It stops. It's officer Peace Spencer. He helps me up. Puts me on the back seat of his police car. Drives me home. I would have been better off going to jail. He tells my mom he found me on the side of the highway, and it looks like my arm is broken. He's already called Dr. Eklund, our town doctor, who is waiting at the clinic for us. She thanks him. He drives off. She then gives me a good licking and takes me to the clinic. There's the doc. He treats me as best he can and tells her to take me to the hospital. That cranks her up even more. More lickings. Then she finds out, Dr. Eklund and his wife were having their anniversary dinner when he got called out at the Waimea Hotel. More of you know what. My poor bike got no attention for months, but I did.

Hamakua Sugar Trucks

Monday through Friday, bulk sugar tractor trailers, would pass through Waimea on their way to Kawaihae from Hamakua, to unload raw sugar to be shipped to California into table sugar and other products for cooking or baking. Sugar was a major component of our economy, a component we thought would be here forever. Sugar was king once. Pineapple its queen. Both are dead. I miss seeing those trucks rumbling through Waimea on their way to Kawaihae Harbor to be loaded onto tankers bound for Oakland.

Kilauea Iki

You need, in your lifetime, to see one of our friendly volcanoes. We saw one. Kilauea Iki 1968. It was a spectacular, stunning sight to behold. A fountain of magma shooting two thousand feet into the night sky. We stood on the crater's edge and watched Madame Pele, our fire goddess, coughing up lava. Hundreds of us saw all of this in real time and real action. Madama Pele entertained us for an entire month. To hear the gasses hissing, the bombs exploding, observe the hot magma bubbling in a crater sculpted like a pot, the yellow, red and orange fountain in the form of a Christmas tree, illuminating the night sky, see new earth being created, smell the stench of sulfur. He inoa no, no Pele.

Ninth grade 1962-63

My grandpa and dad died. It was a sad year. Two good men I loved, both of whom I have fond memories of. It was a happy year to. Honor Roll (entire year). Student body president. School paper Editor (Bronco Script). Graduation year end ceremony voted Most Studious and Most Likely to Succeed with Lillian Kiyota. Got into Kamehameha School for Boys.

Church

Every weekend for years. Mow lawn (cemetery, church, parsonage). Took several hours to do all the mowing. Polish pews. Wash windows. Straighten up classrooms. Sweep and mop floors. Attend Sunday school and church. Grumble. Grumble. Grumble. Total waste of breath. Our ma didn't pay any attention to our grumbles. Rewarded us with more work. We got medals for perfect attendance. Big deal. Used to make church fun in a silly, childish, bearable way. Stuck our tongue at the minister who ratted on us. It was amusing while it lasted until…the old lady yanked us by the ears and dragged us by the ears in front of the entire congregation to sit in the pew between the deacons, in front of the big mouth pastor. I don't think anyone felt sorry for us.

Mr. Mills

He was a special man. Our school janitor. He was nice to us kids. Always carried himself with a smile. One man, he took care of our huge school yard and garden areas. Served the demands of our teachers and administration. Never complained. Focused on all that needed to get done and got it done. As kids, we helped him where we could. Today, too many cry babies who hide behind the union. Don't get me wrong. I'm a pro union guy. In fact, I'm glad to see the unions making a comeback.

Traffic

Very little traffic kid time in Waimea. We could ride our horses on the highway. We moved cattle right on the main highway to our homestead. Cars had to pull off the road. If you were in a rush, you got to your destination late. Population then, (AD 1960), about 1,500. Horses and cattle had priority. Not today. Population today, (AD 2200), about 8000. Traffic is constant. Cars, tractor trailers, motorcycles, cyclists, hikers. Ride a horse on the highway, expect to be stopped by a cop and get ticketed. Our paperboy used to deliver our newspaper and make his collections on horseback. Today, we get our paper virtually. My how the world has changed.

Drying clothes

We had a speed queen washing machine with a roller to help dry the clothes and a line to hang the clothes on to finish the job. We lived where it rained a lot. There were times when the clothes didn't dry, the clothes smelled horrible. Our mom solved the problem by rewashing, putting the clothes in baskets, piling us and the clothes in our mercury. We would go to Spencer Beach Park where it was nice and sunny. Strung ropes from tree to tree. Hung the clothes out to dry. We'd make the ten-mile drive worthwhile. Swim or pole fish. Have lunch. Our mom made the best sardine omelets. The best. We'd have omelets, poi and rice balls. Spent about six hours at Spencer's. When we took the clothes off the lines and folded them. It was like folding paper. They were dry but dead stiff. So, when we got home, out came the ironing board, iron and water in a bowl. No iron free clothes in those days.

Charlie Rose

Charlie was our Police District commander. He and I would sneak off somewhere for coffee practically every morning, where we could not be bothered. Of course, his secretary had her sources, so if he had something important to deal with, she knew where to find us. We'd talk about local and national events.

Once a lady drowned in our harbor. We were first at the scene. Her body was bloated and ready to burst. He tells me to flip the body over. I didn't want to touch it. I say to him, "That's your job. Not mine." Charlie didn't want to touch it either. He says to me. "Ah, let's wait for the cops to show up."

I couldn't believe what he'd tell people and he didn't mess around. One day we come out of court. There's this punky guy who walks up to and starts harassing him. "So, you're a cop. Police commander eh. I've heard you have a rule. A hippie like me must be out of town by sundown." "That's right. You'd better be out of here by sundown." "And if I'm not?" "Stick around and you'll find out." The guy left town.

We helped start a canoe club with several others. We won a regatta in Hilo. It was a big deal. A big win. We came back to our club's headquarters on the beach in Kawaihae. Of course, we had a lot of renegades and troublemakers in our club. That was why we started the club. Help them burn off some of their bad energy. It was early evening. There was marijuana smoke everywhere. I was riding with him in his police car. He looks at me and says, "Robert my man, what we gonna do about this?" I look at him and say, "Nothing. We just gonna go in, join the party and have a good time." We did, soon the air cleared, the smokers disappeared.

He was a great guy and had a tremendous sense of humor. Many times, he gave me treatment plan suggestions for my adult probationers who were thirty possibly forty years older than me. Some could have been my grandpa. His ideas often were better than mine. I was in my twenties, a young punk with a badge working for the court.

We'd get together with two commanders from the adjoining districts to shoot the bull, drink beer and have a few laughs monthly. They'd pick on me and me on them. We met at Charlie's since his home was smack in the middle. We usually met on a Friday evening. This one evening the topic was, "Who's boss?" Captain… starts off and says in his house he's the boss. His wife doesn't tell him what to do. Ten minutes later his wife drives up. "…. get in the car!" What does he do? He gets in the car. We watch them drive off. Charlie looks at me and Commander….. "Guess we know who's boss in ….. house." We died laughing, switched to another topic but could not help thinking about poor Commander ….."

He and his wife were so hospitable and kind to Kathy and our family. Rosie, his wife was a great cook. When he retired from the police department he worked as an investigator for the federal public defender's office. He'd visit me at my Office of Hawaiian Affairs office in downtown Honolulu from time to time. He usually needed help with a project, but we'd always reflect on bygone days and all the fun we had. I miss the man, but he remains in my heart. He always will. Even his wife and kids. Crystal and Kawika are no longer kids. She's a successful lawyer, married to a neat guy and Kawika is a math teacher.

You have friends and dear friends; with me Charlie is in the dear friend's category. I will always have a lot of respect for him. He was an honest, compassionate, intelligent, down to earth guy. What you saw is what you got. His public face was his private face. He trained his men well. Though he was tough and sometimes rough on them, they had a lot of aloha and respect for him. He taught me work discipline without knowing it. He reported in every morning. Went to his desk. Went over his paperwork, phone calls, appointments. Started at the top of his work list, worked downwards. Major things first. I did the same. Applied his process to my probation work and all my other jobs over the years. Worked superbly. My desk was always clean. Delegated what had to be delegated, followed up on what needed attention, immediate or otherwise, did what was my *kuleana* (responsibility). Treated everyone fairly and well.

Leningrad Elarionoff

Leningrad worked under Charlie Rose. He was born and raised here, went to the mainland, San Jose or Santa Cruz, started his cop career there and transferred home to Hawaii. He was tall, handsome, and a by the book guy usually. Made, in the time I knew him two exceptions.

He loved to challenge superiors. Charlie especially. They would have these debates which turned into fierce arguments. I mean fierce. If I happened to be in my office, to end their debate, one of them would interrupt me. "Hey Robert, let's go have coffee someplace. I got to get out of here." If it was Leningrad, it was his house. Charlie, at Nancy's ice cream shop. That was our usual hang out. There was a coffee pot in the station. But that was too close to home, I guess. It was best anyway. They were ready to throw blows.

Either Leningrad's grandpa or great grandpa migrated to Hawaii from Russia to work for Parker, growing potatoes in Waikii. Married a Hawaiian lady and never left. I forget how the story went exactly. Lenny, as I called him was a talented guy. Designed and built his house. Was a mechanic. Played the ukulele and enjoyed singing. On his days off, he went rock hunting. Looking for ancient fishhooks, poi pounders. A few times I went along, reluctantly. I was afraid something terrible would happen. My hands would be paralyzed. Ghosts would show up at our home. He wasn't scared. Assured me all that was hocus pocus, B.S. stuff. He had an intense interest in tools and artifacts made by our ancestors. I think he was looking to create a mini museum. Yes, I was superstitious.

Len had an eye, a sixth sense. Once we came across a konane stone. A rock checkerboard played by the ali'I to help them make decisions. Like going to war. Who was going to be 'top dog.' I was standing right by it and had no idea I was. He put his hands under it and felt around. "Bobby, this is a konane board." It was a flat, huge heavy rock. Weighed probably a ton. We both tried to lift it but gave up before we ended up with hernias. It was a hot day, and we were sweating like goats. Ended up in fact smelling like goats. We could not move it. He asks me if I wanted it. I said 'hell no.' We tried to move it with the help of iron bars and basic physics. The tide was rising. Soon the rock was submerged. He made a map to mark the area. "Bobby, the next time we come, we are going to get this buggah out of here. I'm going to figure out a way to pull it to where we can load it on the back of my truck." The pull was at least sixty yards. I thought he was kidding. A week later we were back.

He had a friend weld a two-inch-thick pipe sled. With the sled, jacks and steel cables, we gently pulled the rock and loaded it on the back of his truck. It was no effort. Driving home, he asked if I was sure about not wanting the rock. It was a beautiful sunny day. "Len, as sure as the sky is blue and the sun is shining. It's all yours." He was a guy with an iron mind. He was cop, fisherman, carpenter, musician mechanic, gardener, churchman. As a cop, he knew all the hooligans in our area and guaranteed them, if they kept up their mischief, he was going to nab them. After he retired, Lenny served on our County Council. He was not popular with folks. Had a job to do and he was going to do his best at whatever he got his hands on and put his mind to. Like Charlie, I miss him. He was a friend, mentor, confidant.

Letters from ma

My mom wrote me a letter every week for the three years when I was in high school on Oahu. The Kamehameha School for Boys. She never missed a week and every so often would replenish my supply of envelopes and stamps. Many a time I could sense she was lonely. Especially when my brother joined me in my junior year. It was just her, all alone in that big house on Chesbro Lane. Her letters usually carried a Bible verse and the same four reminders. Study hard. Listen to your teachers. Say your prayers. Honor our family. One was different from all the rest which I should have kept. I'm sorry now I threw it away.

John Pea

John was another cop friend. He was the opposite of Leningrad. Len would give his mom, a speeding ticket if she was speeding. He operated under the 'no one is above the law' doctrine. John and I became buddies through my probation work. Our kids needed activities to keep their hands busy and out of trouble. We weren't going to let the devil get near them. Boxing. Basketball. Football. He was there to help hustle money, supply uniforms, chase trophies, find inspirational speakers to talk to the kids.

I could never figure out John. The guy had huge arms and legs. John was tough as an ox, a friend to all. Never heavy bodied people. If he ran for mayor. John would have been elected. But his calling was to be a community policing cop. He felt badly if he had to make an arrest, issue a citation, even a warning to someone. And he served his calling well. John converted bad guys to good guys via his kind, gentle way. John was a rare guy. He didn't need to rough anyone up. His 'velvet glove' was enough to achieve what he needed to do.

The old homestead

Ben (my brother) and I miss dearly the old home stead where we were raised. And at times sadly. That's the only place we knew growing up with Mauna Kea Mountain as our front yard. Tons of memories live there still. But times change and we had to flow with the times. Left the place because of zoning policy. Could not split it in two. Half for him and his family. Half for me and mine. Thankfully, we had options. When our grandpa bought the place in the 1930's, he paid $37 an acre. Today an acre sells for a hundred thousand and rising. It's disgusting. I could write a book about my memories, but I'll spare you. Enough about me. I hope I've provided you a template to work from and some inspiration to write about your own memories to pass down to your kids and them to theirs.

Earl Bakken

I had the wonderful privilege of knowing Earl. Earl invented the pacemaker and lived on our island for many years. And as a philanthropist he had a tremendous aloha for Hawaiian people. He gave a fair amount of his wealth towards Hawaiian education and health. I loved visiting with him, and he always gave me a ton of books to read. Many of them were way above my head.

2016 The Year that was.

As one who does not like to fly;

1. Represented Hawaii at the Cook Islands 50th anniversary year of Independence from New Zealand. It was sad to see cemeteries and homes along the shoreline sinking into the sea. All the result of climate change and global warming. To hear the Prime Minister talk about floating islands as a solution saddened me. Why? The industrial nations of the world have destroyed his nation and are not lending a hand to help.

2. The return of a priceless feather cloak, King Kalaniopu'u presented to Captain Cook in 1779 over two centuries ago from Tepapa Museum in New Zealand to the Bishop Museum in Hawaii. The cloak is made of millions of small bird feathers. How our people wee able and had the patience to string this together mystifies me. Memories I will remember forever.

Japanese neighbors

Good people I will always remember. The Okuras & Wakayama's especially.

Mentors

I had the best of mentors; Circuit Judges, Nelson Doi, Benjamin Menor, Shunichi Kimura at Judiciary. General Manager Anthony Sereno and President Michael Chun at Kamehameha Schools. Trustees Oswald Stender, Boyd Mossman, Kama Hopkins and Kuhio Lewis at the Office of Hawaiian Affairs. My parents, My brother Benjamin. Intelligent, kind, compassionate, hardworking, caring, committed men who helped me along my path and on whose shoulders I stand. Dedicated all to the welfare of the people of Hawaii.

Kathy

My forever memory. My first and only love.

WISHES

WISHES:

One of my favorite **Wishes** songs is by Ann Murray, 'If I could have Three Wishes.' It's a Christmas song I listen to throughout the year, not just during holidays. Why? Because like Ann, I believe in peace, joy and love in all I do.

I wish I took care of my health. I had a hemorrhagic stroke just over five years ago. I'm recovering but it's been a slow process. To cope and help with my recovery, I listen to music. A lot of music. Elvis, Bobby Goldsborough, Glenn Campbell, John Denver, Ann Murray, The Seekers, Bee Gees. To name a few.

I can't do much these days but sit at my computer and write with my index finger after the four nerve meds I'm on fog out and the little energy I have within to work with. Take some advice from me, please. I'm one of these fortunate dummies, God has given a second chance. Take care of yourself. Employ moderation. Eat well. Run. Jump rope. Ride a bike. Stay active, physically, mentally, spiritually. Be kind. Be happy. Be positive. Sing. Laugh a lot. Have fun. Spend time with others.

I wish I could wind the clock back sixty-five years. I'd do many things differently. Focus on my health especially. I should have taken better care of this vessel God has given me. I was off to a bad start when I was born in 1948 and suffered a stroke in 2016 at age 66.

I wish I attended my university graduation, but I refused to walk. Now I wish I did. It was my mom's dream. By not walking I denied her that dream. Her family came out of the taro patch in Waimanu Valley. In the shift from the ancient ways to western education, western education was important to her. She was living her dream through me. I was her hope, and, in my selfishness, I denied her that dream.

I wish I returned to church as my mom requested. I didn't. I think she felt lonely, sitting Sunday after Sunday by herself in the pew our family sat in for years. My dad was gone, my brother was gone and so was I.

I wish I had not trusted people as much as I did. I got screwed by a few.

I wish I went to community college rather than the university. I prefer working with my hands and less with my head.

I wish I listened to myself more than others regarding my future. I was so docile and let others tell me what I should be.

I wish when we went into farming, we did orchard farming. It would have been easier to manage, less work, less costly although it would have taken a lot longer to see a return on investment.

I wish I could fly to the moon. Watching it rise and fall nightly is not enough for me.

I wish we'd spend more on education, schools than on building bombs and prisons. Common, practical, human sense.

I wish I could play the piano. I love piano music and enjoy watching Jason Coleman's show.

I wish I could surf. Lived in the islands and never learned to catch waves on a long board.

I wish our dog Monty was still around. He was a dear friend.

I wish I was still healthy so I could teach our grandsons how to hit a baseball. I was once a batting coach.

I wish I could raise chickens, especially hens like when I was a kid, and steal their eggs. Fun, fun, fun.

I wish my Lindsey grandpa was still around so our four grandsons could sit at his feet and hear his stories, both fact and fiction. And watch him play the piano. Grandsons should know and learn from their great grandparents. Conversation is a great way to bridge worlds, generations.

I wish I could spend an evening with Elvis just 'talking story.' I'm like stories and I know he'd have much to tell.

I wish I could walk across the Golden Gate Bridge on a sunny day with Kathy. For me, the bridge is a great achievement and to walk it with Kathy, a native San Franciscan would be the ultimate achievement.

I wish I could spend a day with Thoreau on Walden Pond. I've read his book and would love to have a 'heart to heart' chat with him about it.

I wish I was wise like the owl. I envy people with wisdom.

I wish I had wings and could fly like a bird from tree to tree.

I wish I was an elf in Santa's workshop. That would be great fun making toys for Santa to put on his sleigh.

I wish I could meet Queen Lili'uokalani and converse with her about the 1893 overthrow. How the rug was pulled out from under her by a coup led by U.S. Minister Stevens and U.S. marines. How her Kingdom was stolen from her by the U.S.

I wish I could see another John Denver concert at the Waikiki Shell. I love his music, Kathy and I enjoyed his first one at the Shell on a warm, moonlight evening. To see the moon rising over Leahi was stunning. A night we will never forget.

I wish I could attain Eagle Scout. A dream I never accomplished.

I wish I could be a tattered Bible. To be the most read book in the world.

I wish I could explore the depths of the Mariana Trench. Just to learn what lurks in its depths.

I wish a cure for COVID will be found soon. Every month a new variant appears to be emerging.

I wish the Ukraine War would end so the rest of the world can rest in peace. Who knows what Putin will do? His threat might become reality. He looks like a caged rat. A danger to the world.

I wish every country in the world with nuclear and other weapons of war would get rid of their arsenals. What a waste of resources which can be better spent on things more useful to humanity.

I wish every community had an ice cream and snow cone shoppe. A neat place for kids to hang out.

I wish I was at Kitty Hawk when the Wright brothers launched their plane. They had no idea how their invention would change the world.

I wish I was buddy buddy with Henry Ford and able to thumb a ride on his 'horseless carriage.' Imagine, riding with the man who invented the carriage.

I wish I knew Nelson Mandela and Desmond Tutu personally. I've only met them through articles and books.

I wish I could have met my pure Hawaiian grandpa personally and heard his stories. He lived in a different time. While Hawai'i was still a sovereign kingdom.

I wish I could have a 'heart to hear' visit with my favorite mentors. My parents of course. Circuit Judge Nelson Doi. For the first time I ran into a buzz saw. I could not cruise and get away with it.

Regrets

REGRETS:

Frank Sinatra croons one of many songs that made him famous. The song I love is 'I Did It My Way.' The word **REGRETS** is embedded in it. And like Frank I too have just a fistful of **REGRETS.**

I regret that I didn't attend my university graduation in 1970. That would have made my mom very, very happy. She was living a dream through me because she didn't have much in the way of formal education. This is my greatest regret. Denying, depriving, robbing her of her dream, after all she sacrificed for me.

She wanted me to return to church. I said I would but not until years later. Fifty-two to be exact.

I regret I threw the letter she sent me when I was in high school about what eventually would become our annual Merrie Monarch Festival away. The Super Bowl of Hula in the world. It's a beautiful festival of dance, music, choreography, lei, flowers and much else. Folks come to our island in April to witness the best of hula. Its televised globally also. Our mom went to the first festival over fifty years ago. Her letter was about fifteen pages. And a beautiful letter.

The kind of letter that put me in the front row at the event. At the feet and graceful arms of the dancers. I could sense the fragrance of the flowers and ferns. Hear the pounding of the *pahu* (drums) by the *kahu* (masters), hear their kahea (calls), feel the *mana* (power, electricity) of the place in which it was held. Today, the festival is a MAJOR event. The founders had no idea what they started.

Neither did I. I read the letter. Said to myself. "This is nice." And tossed it in the trash can. Now I wish I kept it.

I regret not being serious about school and college. I was on cruise control, did just enough to get by and didn't make full use of the opportunities offered. Was I a 'slacker? Yes.

I should have listened to Kathy more instead of being so ……. mule headed. I would have been in better shape today. I know what my dad would have said. "You're so smart, you're stupid."

I regret not learning how to dance. Kathy is a beautiful dancer. Now, I can't ask her to save the last dance for me.

I regret not giving my health the priority it deserved. So here I sit in a wheelchair and everyday I'm tired from doing nothing.

The party was fun. Huff had a grand time. He ate the *menpachi* like there was not going to be a tomorrow. He quizzed me several times. "You didn't let our secret out, did you?" "Of course not." "That's my boy. Used my net, I hope?" "Yep. Used your net!"

It was about 10 o'clock and the moon was directly above us. Staring down at us. "Huff, where's your chick?" "I'm turning her in for a chicken."

"Really!" "Really?" "Really! You were right. She was just trying to pick my pockets." "Ah, that's too bad." "Yeah, Bea was special. Like Kathy. I sure miss Bea. Her goodness. Smile. Patience. You know how she was. I miss how we used to sit around the breakfast table in the morning. We'd laugh. Joke. Kid each other. You know the saying, 'Your first love is your true love.' It's true." "I agree. She sure was a special lady. Like Kathy. Yes, she was. I miss Bea too. Her sweet smile. Her kindness. Her pies. Bread pudding. Her laugh." Then there was a gap in our conversation. Things went silent for a few minutes. He was looking at the moon in complete wonderment. Finally, I decide to break the silence. "Otherwise, how are you doing, Huff?" "Great. Just great. Thanks for the wonderful party." "It was an honor for us to do it for you, after all you've done for us. An honor." "Got a favor to ask of you. A small one, Huff." "Of course, anything you want. What's on your mind, Pops?" "I want you to drive me home tonight. We'll talk about it on the way." "Of course. But you got to ride Rusty." "Now, I have not rode that truck of yours in years. It will be a treat." "There are a few holes in the floor. Small ones." "I think I can handle that." He calls his driver over and tells Rudy I'm taking him home. "In that calamity." "Of course. Why not?" "As you wish, Sir. As you wish. See you in the morning." "Huff, I want to talk to you about something special. Real special."

We get in Rusty. "I love this heap of rust, Huff. It brings back many good memories."

"So where do you want me to take you?" "To the harbor."

"Place is shut down for the night." "I got the key to the gate." He dangles a bunch of keys in front of me. 'How'd you get it?" "When you know Al Capone, you can get anything. Anything!" I do as he says. Drive up to the main gate. "Here open the gate and lock it after you." "Now what?" "Drive to slip 76." I do as he instructs. "What do you see, my man?" "I see a huge firkin yacht. Whoever owns that boat must own a bunch of oil wells in Texas." "Guess what?" "What?" "It's yours and Kathy's." "You're kidding?" "Huff, you know, I'm not one to kid around." "That thing must have cost you millions." "Now Huff, that's none of your business. Your job is to go around the world with Kathy and help me live out a longstanding **memory,** a longstanding **wish** and resolve a longstanding **regret** to Bea, okay! Something that's been bugging me for a long, long time." "What's that?" "Go around the world." "But she did." "Yes, but she wanted me to go with her." "And you didn't." "That's right. I didn't and I should have." "Too late for that now. So now I want to make it up to her through you and your bride, okay." "OKAY." "I'll give you a personal tour of **BEA** in the morning. It's outfitted and staffed completely. All you both must do is get your passports and enjoy the cruise." "Aren't you coming along?" "Heck no! I got better things to do." "Like what?" "Play bridge and hang out with Joe and Frank. Plus, I ain't got much gas left in my tank and the pistons in my engine haven't been pounding too well lately." He laughs. "Thanks for everything. You and Willow made my night. Get me home. I gotta get to bed. And do Willow a favor." "Like what?" "Donate Rusty to the church. Your new one is parked in your garage." "What!" "But what…" "I love Rusty." "Take Rusty on the cruise with you, Huff. There's a garage on the boat. Take him with you and dump him in the China Sea or the Atlantic. Make Willow happy. Quit being a jackass and grow up. Take good advice from one good jackass to another."

The moon was at high midnight. I look up at the man in the moon. He's looking down at us. Smiling widely. Agreeing with the Pops. "I'll think about it. I'll think about it. You know what Huff? Got a better idea. See this pipe." "For as long as I've known you. Yes!" "As you never would give up Rusty, I'll never give up this pipe." "Why not?" "It's part of me is. So, I completely understand where you're coming from." "I'm glad you understand, Huff." "Let's make a deal." "Depends on what the deal is. I'm all ears." "Joe's grandson owns a body upholstery shop or whatever you call it." "I've seen his sign on the road to Waimea but never been in the shop." "While you and Willow are on cruise I'll have Rusty worked over. All the holes patched up. Repaint him from top to bottom. What color?" "Rose red." "The engine overhauled so he doesn't belch and cough anymore. Maybe replaced if need be." "No, please don't alter the engine." "The inside reupholstered. Give Rusty a complete makeover. The entire 'ten yards.' How does that sound?" "Sounds like music to me. Where'd your inspiration, idea come from so quickly?" "See that guy sitting on his butt looking down at us?" "You mean the Man in the Moon?" "The Man in the Moon. He whispered to me. I got the idea from him. Take a good look. He's ready to cast a net. I think he's going fishing for *menpachi*.

He's got to catch five fish and a few loaves of bread. I hear Jesus is dropping by, so he needs to play host to a few thousand believers. He's having his own Woodstock, but only Hawaiian music allowed."

"Huff, I like your idea about Rusty. And you do need some sleep. Next, you'll be talking about saving Social Security, Medicare, and Medicaid." He laughs, puffs on his pipe. "I've been blessed, Huff. Really blessed. And I want you to know you have been a big part of it."

www.ingramcontent.com/pod-product-compliance
Lightning Source LLC
LaVergne TN
LVHW040200080526
838202LV00042B/3244